PRAISE FOR
INEVITABLE LOSS OF INNOCENCE

A beautifully written coming of age story that hits all the right notes. This short novel by Zara Macias marks the debut of a brilliant new voice. Macias' debut covers the well-trodden ground of a college student being away from home for an extended period for the first time in writing that is almost elegiac. The author's deft use of language helps immerse the reader in the narrator's experience, giving the events of the story an up close and personal ambience.

Shawn Johal | CEO | Elevation Leaders

The Inevitable Loss of Innocence represents a powerful debut by author Zara Macias. She combines elements of a bildungsroman with a keen sense of the modern college experience to pen a gripping story of the challenges encountered by a "Kentucky girl" of Mexican heritage struggling to adapt to the rarefied world of a high-profile Washington DC-based university. Her limited financial resources pose a challenge for living the "high life" some of her fellow students have the funds to pursue. On the romantic front, her desire for a meaningful relationship, however characterized, is challenged by the more casual attitude preferred by, one imagines, many young men these days. Overall, a highly readable take on the modern college experience from the standpoint of a passionate, intelligent, and principled young woman.

Tamara Nall | CEO & Founder, The Leading Niche

THE INEVITABLE LOSS OF INNOCENCE

From Girl to Real World

Zara Macias

Copyright © 2023 Zara Macias
Published in the United States by Story Leaders.
www.leaderspress.com

All rights reserved. No part of this book may be reproduced or transmitted in any form or by any means, electronic or mechanical, including photocopying, recording, or by an information storage and retrieval system – except by a reviewer who may quote brief passages in a review to be printed in a magazine or newspaper – without permission in writing from the publisher.

All trademarks, service marks, trade names, product names, and logos appearing in this publication are the property of their respective owners.

ISBN 978-1-63735-192-5 (Amazon pbk)
ISBN 978-1-63735-193-2 (ebook)

Library of Congress Control Number: 2023908481

For my mother— Anna Rose Murguia Preciado

A cautionary tale with difficult truths.

The one you would've handed to me prior to the move. Grateful for the opportunity to pay it forward for all the young women interested in elite schools. To share the story that's often unspoken.

Fairytales don't prepare young women with big dreams and modest origins.

CONTENTS

Chapter 1. Introduction 7

Chapter 2. White University 8

Chapter 3. Blaze 11

Chapter 4. Roommate No. 1, Elena 19

Chapter 5. New York 22

Chapter 6. The Bench at White University 30

Chapter 7. Disconnecting from Elena 32

Chapter 8. The New Yorker 36

Chapter 9. The Night Before 38

Chapter 10. Second Trip to New York 40

Chapter 11. Message I Have for the New Yorker 46

Chapter 12. Trust 48

Chapter 13. District 1 54

Chapter 14. Going Back to District 12 57

Chapter 15. Weight 58

Chapter 16. Revisiting Blaze 60

Chapter 17. Crazy Time in History 64

Chapter 18. The History Buff 65

About Zara Macias 70

INTRODUCTION

On August 20, 2016, a Kentucky girl settles into the prestigious capital of the United States. A ' Kentucky girl...' What does that label reflect? Some people may picture the preacher's daughter swaying in a white dress and cowboy boots, yeehaw! A few here and there know of the Kentucky Derby. Some recognize the legendary Muhammad Ali's hometown of Louisville, Kentucky. Everyone—and I mean everyone—will mention the damn fried chicken.

Let's try this again—August 20, 2016, a girl leaves home. She does not expect or encounter anything negative upon arrival, although she quickly recognizes it is easy to feel out of place at White University—unless, of course, you have lived in twelve different countries and vacationed in the Galapagos Islands.

I know the title of this book leads people to assume the loss of an overamplified concept—virginity. In this context, losing innocence involves transitioning from skipping rocks on McNeely Lake to having a man yell, "Hey, pretty lady. Hey, are you listening to me!" as she makes her way down the subway.

WHITE UNIVERSITY

White University intimidates everyone. Their marketing team ensures everyone recognizes their pristine marble buildings, modern embellishments, renowned word-class visitors, and prime DC location.

To be completely honest, my application has been a challenge to their typical student acceptance—white, rich, and out of touch.

When my acceptance letter came in with a $38,000 bonus, the opportunity no longer seemed out of touch. Although, on my first day, I note that there are people who are out of touch.

A frustrated voice in my math class nervously utters, "I don't understand this, do you?"

"Yeah," the girl next to him scoffs.

"How did you do it?" he follows.

"I don't know, I just did," she responds with an eye-roll.

I look over to see who is speaking so discourteously.

The girl. The girl with the cool striped pants. I've met her before class, and she has seemed harmless then—high ponytail and bright smile.

"Cool pants!" I compliment.

"Thanks!" she gloats.

Now she remains stern and persistently looks at her Michael Kors watch. I stop looking at her and focus on the guy.

"Hey, what don't you understand?" I calmly ask.

It doesn't take more than thirty seconds to explain it to him, and he is very gracious afterward.

What I find perplexing is the girl. What does Michael Kors girl have to lose? Her precious time she is monotonously watching? It is unsettling, and I leave class bothered, as in "a rock is in my shoe" bothered.

All right, I'll cut to the chase. Yes, I've met a few boys at White University. I'll list them and cut the suspense: Blaze, the New Yorker, and History Buff. You may think, is this a coming-of-age story? Maybe...but maybe not. More broadly, *The Inevitable Loss of Innocence* will shine a light on the realities of college life. None of the *Legally Blonde* or *Mona Lisa Smile* bullshit. We are talking about the awkward undressing in front of your roommates, wandering into smoke-filled rooms, and lying on the freshly-cut quad grass gulping, "What the hell am I doing here?"

This is also a story of a young woman searching for comfort, love, and joy in an environment that prioritizes power.

As I have alluded in the introduction, this is not just any college. This is the renowned *White* University. On the topic of white . . .

Let me introduce you to Blaze.

BLAZE

Blaze resists calling himself a writer, but...

He's a Writer

His words captivate
Activate my vivid imagination
Humor with a touch of persuasion
I demand he keep writing
An encore for the lady in the
Blue dress and paint marks
Water gardens and honest conversations
Lost in thought, he overthinks
Meanwhile, I feel alive dancing between his introspective expression

Aside from having a writer's soul, I could slap the shit out of Blaze. (And I did...*Sigh*. Wait for the backstory.) Blaze's intellect impresses everyone, and that alone encourages me to look past his general aura of dis-ease. Anyway...

It's the damn eye contact, I swear.

"Attagirl, there you go. Good job," Blaze whispers.

After weeks of sheepishly avoiding eye contact, solid eye contact for a smooth twenty seconds proceeds. His eyes are very soft. No, I don't jab his eye with my index finger and feel it. But they aren't harsh and they aren't sad; they are soft. I adore his pale-green eyes. There is a sense of innocence within Blaze's eyes, the innocence I desperately try to hold on to. *Innocence* being synonymous with "absence of evil "—more accurately, *unawareness* of said evil.

I spend time with Blaze, arguably too much. I can be with Blaze for hours upon hours and never get bored.

He's comforting in an uncomfortable place.

Conversations flow for five hours straight, whether it be in front of a gigantic bowl of pasta or on the steps of the Lincoln Memorial.

One night we overindulge in peach vodka, drunkenly wandering all over the place, and rest in a secluded room with oddly shaped furniture.

Our hands touch, and Blaze tenses up and admits, "Zara, you make me so nervous."

"Nervous?" I say, hesitantly .

He shrugs. "Yeah. "

"Why? " I ask, insistent.

"Because...you're so smart...and you're very attractive."

I guess the peach vodka has me looking at his lips more.

I follow his lead. "You are not so bad yourself."

His nerves are endearing, and peach vodka gives you this inexplicable courage, the courage that prompts you to place your hand over a boy's knee and process. "You don't have to be so nervous."

Then, without any doubt, he glides his hand onto my lower chin and locks his lips with passion. After the third kiss, we both smile and feel each other's teeth. The moment is warm; the moment is soft.

You'll cherish these warm moments and then feel ice-cold when your roommate Elena shouts, "Is that Blaze!"

I squint my eyes to focus my vision amid the foggy darkness and flashing LED lights. I make out a blurry outline of a tall guy making out with a short blond girl in a messy bun. I don't want to believe it's him, so I squint harder to make sure. Yes, that's Blaze.

My blood flows agitation, and I scoff and shake it off. I want to walk over to congratulate the conquest but, midway there, I note the pause and smile after the kiss.

He does that with everyone . . .

My heart hardens like lead, and I muster, "I need a drink."

Nine times out of ten, liquid ' courage' is liquid cowardice.

After a few drinks, I stumble into someone random, and he declares, "Hey, I haven't been able to keep my eyes off of you."

My roommate exclaims, "Blaze is right next to us!"

I lock eyes with Blaze and lean against the random guy and laugh boisterously. Blaze immediately crosses his arms and leans against the wall. I unpin my ponytail and wave my hair and hips simultaneously.

Perhaps that's part of being a college student, creating the illusion of being carefree during heartache.

Drink after drink, we sink deeper and deeper into our pain and then wonder why we wake up feeling like shit.

Blaze's morning texts follow, and I reject him. I want to reject him forever, but around 7:00 p.m. I lose my will and give in to meet.

"Meet me in the library. I don't have time for coffee or lunch," I text back.

He shows up with hickeys all over his neck and clearly shaken up. His voice cracks, and he suggests taking the conversation outside.

I quickly agree.

Fresh air over library basement air any day...

I will never understand why he enjoys the stuffy library basement. We walk in silence as we make our way up the stairs and out the front door. He is having such a hard time speaking.

His throat locks up, but he continues, "I had everything, I would say, planned, but I am going blank now."

He decides to go off script and pours his heart out to me. He insists that the night before, he wasn't who he truly was and, although his friends were saying his actions were acceptable, he says, "They don't understand the connection we have . . ." Above all, he stresses how much he cherishes our friendship.

"Honestly, Zara, I don't know what I would do without you here." His last words echo in my ear.

To be honest, I do not know what I will do without Blaze at White University. When you meet someone here, it involves a socioeconomic breakdown of your persona: What do your parents do? Where do you come from? Have you been to DC before? How are you going to be of use to me?

"My father's a senator."

"My mom administrates at another high-profile university."

"My father collaborates with the FBI and other intelligence agencies."

My mother has been a bank teller for over ten years, and she finally took the entrepreneurial leap recently.

She has dreams, just like me.

It is refreshing when Blaze decides to practice his broken Spanish the first night we meet.

"Aver, cual es tu favorita comida?" I pose. Translation: "Let's see, what's your favorite food?"

"Carne." He grins. Translation: "Meat."

I chuckle because he conveys a general food group rather than a specific dish. I cut him some slack and reveal I am a carnivore myself. All meats sound good to me.

Blaze is...nice. He's just made a mistake; it does not reflect the ' real him.'

After processing Blaze's role in my journey, I slowly release the books I am pressing tightly against my chest and slide closer to him to rest my head on his chest.

"We can stay in touch, but don't hurt me, okay?" I entreat.

Comforting silence follows for about thirty seconds, and then my mind compartmentalizes (typical).

"So, we addressed the platonic feelings, we can put that box away. Now what do we do about the romantic-feelings box?

He chuckles and clarifies, "Are you asking to be exclusive?"

"What? No! You haven't even asked me to be with you. I don't know if we should involve that box or put it in storage."

"I think you are asking if we want to be exclusive, Zara." He smiles and contemplates. "Well, I will try it if you want to try," he decides.

"Yeah, I don't know about that. I have to think about it, okay? Can you give me some time?"

"Sure. Take your time. "

I sit silently in shock, and my eyes wander toward the School of International Service.

"Can I walk you back to your dorm? It's getting dark," Blaze suggests.

"Yeah! Let's go. I have homework to do. "

I stumble into my floor's study hall with a family-sized pack of Oreos and Hershey's nuggets.

"Hellooo, friend," sweet Iris greets me.

"Oh, thank goodness, you can help me eat this chocolate."

Iris does not hesitate. "I can *always* help you eat some chocolate."

I set down my slender iPad and off-brand keyboard and try to focus on my reading questions. I keep resting my pen over my lips, unconvinced.

Iris chimes in. "Girl, you've been reading the same question for the past fifteen minutes. What's distracting you?"

"Ugh, Blaze," I confess. "Stupid Blaze."

I tell her the story of how we met and, as a Brazil native, Iris appreciates the broken Spanish piece and actively listens.

After the elaborate rundown, she advises, "Follow your heart. Love will always be a risk. Everyone deserves a second chance."

Her words resonate, and I text Blaze: "Meet me in the connecting bridge between our dorms."

Our timing synchronous, we see each other walking down the hallway at the same time.

He looks disoriented and slightly worried.

I speed up when we're about ten feet away and grab his collar and push him in between two columns. My grip remains forceful, and I slap him in the face.

His eyes widen, and I lock my lips with his fiercely.

"You're mine, okay?" I snap.

"Yes. Okay," he adds, before gently tilting my chin up for another kiss.

The Inevitable Loss of Innocence

ஐ ஐ ஐ

So what happens next?

Well...

We hug each other more.

We eat maple bacon donuts in the morning.

We take long walks during the day, and at night he spins around in the cool evening air while I sport his musky green jacket.

An encore for the lady in the blue dress and paint marks.

ROOMMATE NO. 1, ELENA

The Inevitable Loss of Innocence

As roommates, it's expected we take part in "Welcome Week" collectively. This week acclimates freshman college students prior to attending classes. The university sponsors a bunch of extravagant events. The events are ridiculous, but at least there aren't any out-of-pocket expenses.

In contrast, Elena keeps wanting to get off campus.

She keeps wanting to take these Ubers into town. After a few days of observing her spending habits, I recognize the need to talk about my financial reality.

"Are you ready? Let's go!" she chirps.

"Hey, Elena, so I don't want to be a party pooper but . . ."

"But what? You don't like ice cream?" she asks.

"Ha, no, I actually love ice cream. It's just…I can't be doing this at the rate we've been going. I must be frugal. You know, I have student loans and…limited funds. I brought extra cash, but…," I mumble.

She resumes, "But you have a limited supply. I get it, well, ha, I don't…My parents just give me a credit card and take care of paying for it. Anyway…how about I pay for the rest of this week and we figure the rest out later?"

An unlimited credit card? That suggests a lot…I don't think she'll ever get it. And I don't want her to pay for my stuff. This doesn't feel right.

Out loud I say smiling, "Um…okay."

Elena has unusual habits.

On a stressful day, she spends over $600 online shopping. She refers to the practice as retail therapy.

She doesn't know how to do her laundry or cook a meal from scratch.

She phrases a lot of her activities in relation to her résumé.

How do you even write a résumé anyway?

Like other students, Elena obsesses over brands, status, and being mindful of how she is going to write her memoir.

On the positive, Elena has a cheerful smile and an infectious laugh. Her intentions are often pure, and I admire her intelligence.

Almost everyone at White University proves to be highly intelligent and well-traveled.

Even in the stuffy basement library, Elena and I spark an interesting conversation with two gals headed to New York for fall break.

"Oh, sweet. Is New York home?" I ask.

"Yes! And it's so cheap to get there from here. You know you can get a round-trip ticket for only fifty bucks in Chinatown?"

Elena and I look at each other with wide eyes . . .

"We have to go," we say simultaneously.

NEW YORK

My roommate, Elena, mentions the trip to her family in a nonchalant manner. My mom's response?

Farrr from nonchalant.

The moment I mention New York, she shouts, "WHAT! Are you crazy? No, no, NO!"

"Mom, calm down. My roommate has been four times! It's safe, I promise."

Long story short, I will not win. Solution?

"Okay, I won't spend the night in New York, Mom, I promise."

Technicallyyy, I have not lied.

We'll leave at seven in the morning and leave at 3:00 a.m. So, I will *not* spend the night in New York.

What? I want to see the United Nations, Central Park, the MET—everything, I wanted to see everything! The bus ticket is only fifty dollars round trip!

Although everyone's conception of New York differs drastically.

Days before the big day, Elena insists we go to The Plaza. The truth? I do not understand what that place is. Blah, blah, blah something about fancy tea. It sounds bougie, which is fun, I guess.

My best friend, Phoenix, once told me if he had to dedicate a hashtag to me, it would be #BougieOnABudget.

Phoenix recognizes my ability to make a ten-dollar dress look like it's worth one hundred dollars.

Important note—having excellent taste and class has nothing to do with how rich you are.

The Plaza, however, sounds *bougie bougie*, not #BougieOnABudget. I know it isn't feasible for me, but she is *sooo* insistent. Eventually, Elena gets fed up with my wavering and offers to pay.

Daisy, my growing friend a couple of doors down from my dorm, is baffled by my hesitation to let her pay.

"Fuck...just let her pay, whatever."

Daisy cusses a lot. She's from Seattle and wears silky lingerie-esque tops when we go out, so she broadcasts bad-bitch energy.

The scenario is torturous. I don't want to let my roommate down, but deep down, it isn't my style. Deep down, I know who I am. My turf?

The Kentucky State Fair.

Deep-fried Oreos and chocolate-covered cheesecake on a stick.

Warm derby pie with a scoop of vanilla bean ice cream.

Live music and roller-coaster hair.

The Inevitable Loss of Innocence

My response to Elena is, "Okay, sounds fun!"

I cannot lie: The Plaza is breathtakingly beautiful. I get the hype but, also, I wonder if Elena has eaten fried Girl Scout cookies…

As we finish our tea and crumpets, she continues to insist on the drink idea from earlier.

"Since I'm paying for the tea, you can pay for the drinks, right?" she proposes.

I feel super bad for saying no, but I shouldn't be spending money on this. How bad can it be? Forty bucks?

Outwardly, I say, "Um, sure, yeah! No problem!"

"And since you have more confidence, order it, Zara! They'll believe you," she claims.

It is obvious we are underage...but we are in New York, everyone's a hustler...An expensive lesson to learn.

On the menu, the drink "serves two."

What does the server do?

He brings two drinks that can serve two, *each*.

Total? Sixty-five dollars times two, plus tax—$140 for two friggin' drinks...

Well...

Shit.

I become a worried mess when I see the bill. Elena rolls her eyes and insists I calm down. She cannot comprehend the situation.

I want us to be happy, but since when does happiness involve getting drunk at some swanky hotel at two in the afternoon?

Happiness involves a feeling, not a location.

"It's fine, Zara. I mean, it already happened. What are you going to do?"

I cannot help but flashback to the moment we had a heart-to-heart conversation about my fragile financial situation and her unlimited credit card.

"It is fine, Zara. I mean, it already happened. What are you going to do?"

Yeah, what am I going to do? *I should have said no.* I should have been true to myself. I should have been responsible. A drink is fun, but the price is abnormal. As we learn in economics, the cost does *not* outweigh the benefit for me. I don't walk into swanky hotels and indulge in macaroons, mini sandwiches, and English breakfast tea.

My friends back home would laugh in my face for acting this way.

Rather than responding to her comment, I nod and smile. I put everything I have to my name in a shiny, gold-edged checkbook. The pompous waiter swings by minutes later and forces me to release the booklet.

He locks his chestnut-colored eyes with mine and utters, "Thank you, senorita," with his annoying grating tone.

Ugh, he reveals his *paisa* status...How could he do this to his own people?!

I guess that is what I get for pretending to be a rich *gringa*.

I shake it off and tell myself, *Well, this doesn't have to ruin New York.*

The rum temporarily numbs my distress at the endless round of Ubers.

"Why don't we just take the subway, Elena?" I murmur.

"Oh my gosh, no, Zara. That takes too much time! We have an itinerary!" she declares.

Lane would surely take us to places via subway. Lane is an old friend and a current student at NYU. Lane and I have never been super-close, but he is from my hometown, and I think it will be nice to meet up with someone from home.

A joke circles back home that Lane personifies a traitor. Many resent him because my hipster high school consists almost entirely of rejects from the most elite public high school in Louisville. There's solidarity in the "reject" status. Lane rejects this solidarity and reapplies after freshman year, gets in, and transfers to this elite school.

The hipster high school has rigorous academic programs, beautiful landscaping, and a diverse student body—from varying socioeconomic backgrounds to different ethnic cultures. It is a great school, and it is the best of the best.

Lane lives in a rough neighborhood and constantly strategizes ways to get out of it. And what better way to get into an elite college than by going to one of the most elite high schools?

Sure, he'll miss the hipster high school, but he knows the elite school will help him get into an elite university more swiftly. The elite high school is the better choice in the long term. Smart kid.

Lane always walks with caution and neatly combs his red hair. He supports immigrant-owned coffee shops and volunteers at a refuge ministry.

Perhaps not the best person to try to sneak into a bar/club in New York...He isn't a true New Yorker (at least not yet).

He does not know which clubs will look the other way for a couple of bucks. Plus, Blaze is the only one with a fake ID.

Oh yeah! We meet up with Blaze because he is also in New York for fall break. Whenever he gets the chance, he visits his remarkable sister who's a writer in New York City. I love listening to him talk about her. He speaks fondly and extensively about her talent, enthusiasm, and internal beauty. I really want to meet her; she sounds fabulous.

Anyway, back to the story. After wandering hopelessly around the random streets of New York, we pass a CVS, and Blaze offers to buy us a bunch of cheap wine. Elena and I shrug our shoulders and agree. We're kind of out of options...

As we sip our overly sugary wine, we all say what we want to do with our lives. Everyone's ideas are big and ambitious, except Blaze's...His ideas? Well, he doesn't have any. He is honest. He doesn't know what he is doing. It probably isn't easy for him to be in that room...

As I put myself in his shoes, that moment must have been rough. A few nerdy, ambitious people talking about their grandiose dreams and aspirations while Blaze is still finding himself.

After we have enough sugary light-pink liquid, we say our goodbyes, and Elena and I make our way back to DC.

We instantly crawl into our beds after we buzz in our room key. By the time Elena finishes climbing up the bunk bed stairs, I have fallen into a deep sleep.

The next morning, Elena does not waste time counting the Uber receipts from our trip.

"Okay, it looks like you owe me sixty dollars," Elena remarks.

My eyes widen with disbelief. Sixty bucks? I reposition my debt and ask her to be mindful of the drink mishap.

"Hey, Elena, do you think you could subtract the double ch —"

Before I could explain the mental logic, Elena sternly asserts, "You knew what you were getting yourself into. We both agreed to go to The Plaza and that you'd pay for the drinks. So no, I'm sorry."

"Yes, that's fine. Just give me a moment to figure out how to make the electronic transfer."

To be honest, I have twelve bucks in my bank account, and so I must message my mom a painful lie: "Hey, Mom, I need money for groceries. Could you please send me fifty dollars? That'll cover this month."

It does not take more than two minutes for my mom to agree.

"Yes, *mija*, of course. I love you. Eat well. Let me know if it's enough."

The guilt is crawling up my throat like a furry tarantula.

"Sent," I notify Elena and grab my phone and backpack.

"I sent it on that Venmo app like you asked," I confirm.

"Thanks," Elena responds.

THE BENCH AT WHITE UNIVERSITY

Two days later

Knock, knock.

Blaze waits patiently behind the door. I swing the door open and smile wide at his presence. I was ready to vent about the whole tea drama in New York.

Blaze comes from a wealthy background, but he is not oblivious to the concept of money. He recognizes some people have more than others, but...

Money emphasizes the man-made...incapable of magnifying the real.

He put on a nice red polo. I rarely see him in polos. He is more of a T-shirt guy.

"Hey!" I exclaim.

He seems a little off, but I don't read too much into it. I am ready to spill the tea (no pun intended—okay...maybe it's totally intended).

"Oh my gosh, you will not believe what I got into with Elena..."

I could tell Blaze's mind is fixated on something else when I dramatically explain everything that has happened.

He seems nervous, but perhaps he's just tired from the traveling. He's stayed in New York longer than Elena and me.

Eventually, we arrive at a bench, and I scoot closer to him. After venting my heart out, I think about his sister.

As I lay my head on his chest, I think, *His sister's apartment is probably way cooler than the dumb Plaza. Her apartment is close to the UN too. I know Blaze would have taken me to a local coffee shop rather than Starbucks.*

I could be myself around him...That's enough for him.

Eumoirous—happiness that results from being honest and wholesome.

As I sit on the bench, I think about how it is easy to share eumoirous with Blaze: long strolls, shared french fries, and grocery runs.

Shortly after my thoughts, Blaze utters, "Zara, I need to get something off my chest."

"Yes," I acknowledge.

He gulps. "I can't be exclusive with you anymore."

I straighten up and move away from him.

Oh, that was unexpected. What did I do wrong?

"I mean, I don't know how you feel, but I just had to tell you, I can't do this anymore."

Suddenly, the air becomes colder, my heart becomes heavier, and my throat becomes tighter.

Damn. Say something. Quick.

"It doesn't matter how I feel. You just told me how you feel, and I just have to accept it," I respond.

DISCONNECTING FROM ELENA

After the conversation with Blaze on the bench, I tell Elena. She chuckles out of disbelief and gives me some space.

If only I had read Don Miguel Ruiz's *Four Agreements* at the time. My family has never taught me the first agreement:

Be impeccable with your word.

Instead, my family emphasizes that actions speak louder than words. What you *do* outweighs what you say, think, or contemplate.

Elena is the queen of meticulous expression. She once told me I should keep a journal because "you never know when you will write a memoir."

In Elena's eyes, she's destined for greatness and basking in the public eye, both of which require being meticulous with your words...

Elena belongs in DC.

Or as Dennis Miller gives insights, "Washington, DC, is to lying what Wisconsin is to cheese."

In reality, humans are not meticulous and perfect and destined for greatness.

We are all messy, imperfect, kind of crazy, and great because of that.

Rather than lie to Elena and repress my feelings about the unexpected turn of events with Blaze, I let it *alll* out.

In the comfort of my 150-square-foot dorm, I roar. I stab my vanilla bean ice cream with my marked spoon and vent to Elena endlessly until my body feels calm. She agrees with everything I say and scoffs at intervals.

Elena does not approve of me going out with other friends more frequently, however. I begin partying with Daisy and dancing until my feet get sore.

One day Elena has had enough of my outings and asks, "Why don't you just go out to a nice dinner or something rather than party every week? It's not like you to party."

Inwardly, I think, *Hmm, Elena, let's break this down. What makes up a 'nice' dinner? Does it involve $150 mini sandwiches and a $60 pot of tea? Can I go to this 'nice' dinner in something other than designer wear? Don't you think our dining hall buffet proves to be pretty 'nice'? Oh yeah, our ridiculously overpriced meal plan covers it pretty nicely!*

Out loud, I say, "Thanks for the advice, bye."

I do not want to explain my financial situation to Elena for the third time. I do not want to be in the situation she put me in when we went to New York.

I distance myself from Elena, not out of spite but out of protection. She does not understand my financial circumstances, and it's not something she can load onto her online cart of purchases.

When you first meet your roommate in college, you think you will be best friends. You plan your matching Halloween costumes and meet for lunch every day.

Important note—they may not be your best friend, but they will always be your roommate.

You should always respect and be mindful of your roommate's needs.

Once Elena and I begin drifting as friends, I cannot stand her behavior as a roommate.

She leaves her sweaty gym clothes "to dry" on our bunk bed rather than buy a laundry hamper to conceal the odor. (Yes, I remind her over and over to buy the hamper.)

She spills makeup on our shared dresser.

Most annoying of all, she keeps nagging at my social habits.

The frustrations may sound petty, and they are. The root of the problem, or my authentic hurt, comes from the realization:

I cannot afford to be Elena's friend. Sadly, emotional distance allows financial distance.

Although I can't distance myself from her in our Foreign Policy / Democracy seminar. As our friendship rifts deepen, we become snippier with each other during lecture discussions.

THE NEW YORKER

I am an optimist; I like to think people are naturally good. Perhaps that's why I'm one of only two people in our seminar to favor Hudson's developmental democracy model. The developmental model has faith in humanity and ignores the irony of our self-loathing, capitalist existence. The model assumes people are civically virtuous. Even the New Yorker, a computer science and economics major, I assume to be civically virtuous.

We meet at a Jell-O-shot-filled Halloween party. Romantic, I know.

Over the loud music and sweaty bodies, he describes his stock market successes and recent return to college after taking a gap year.

I tell myself he's had a revelation and came to college to make himself a more informed, virtuous citizen. *Eye-roll...I know.*

His studies are not necessarily wicked undertakings, but most people majoring in these fields are not gung-ho about promoting human rights or being civically engaged.

"Interesting," I respond in a room full of LED lights and smoke machines.

Blaze also took a gap year, but he was is in Argentina through a cool international service program. He always affirms how the gap year has helped him gain a lot of life momentum.

Zara, stop thinking about Blaze and focus on the new guy.

I smile at the New Yorker and illuminate his ambition. This New Yorker seems to be the opposite of Blaze, so he can't hurt me like Blaze, right?

Rather than sitting on the steps of the Lincoln Memorial and talking about our simple comforts, The New Yorker is pushing me against a wall after he gets me heavily intoxicated.

No red flags, right?

Okay, let me rewind.

Again, it's Halloween.

The moment we make eye contact, he approaches me.

"Hey, what's your name?" he says confidently.

Impressed by his direct approach, I become immediately infatuated.

After drinking the drinks he gives me, I make him my ideal guy. His dark-brown eyes are suddenly my favorite color. His intelligence is superior, and his drive—immaculate. More importantly, he is the opposite of Blaze.

When he pushes me against the wall and kisses me, I call it passion. When he props me up on a kitchen counter, I call it passion. When he asks me if I want to have sex with him, I call it love. He asks me to make love to him.

I decline. It's the second day I have ever seen this guy! I can't possibly be in love with him.

I was not in love, but I was still impulsive.

I buy my train ticket to New York two weeks after the night I met him, but I don't buy the ticket to see him. I buy the ticket to escape the feelings I felt the night before.

THE NIGHT BEFORE

I slip on a fitted animal-print Zara dress (yes, Zara like the store) and pair it with a smoky- eye and subtle- nude lipstick. We all take two shots of vodka and lock arms as we make our way down to this mysterious jungle party. I buzz loudly when Daisy grabs my attention.

"Zara, don't make an enormous deal about it, but he's right behind you."

"*Who?*" I exclaim and look back immediately.

Blaze.

I haven't seen him in almost a month.

I laugh hysterically out of nerves, and a wave of insecurity hits me. I pull one girl aside and ask, "Do I look okay? I don't look slutty, do I?"

"You look fine!" she assures.

Am I seriously slut-shaming myself? For what, doofus Blaze? That kid can't give two shits about me. He's even given me the stereotypical "It's not you, it's me" spiel after he announces his inability to remain exclusive.

A thunderstorm of emotions builds up the longer I look at him. A flood of memories comes back. Particularly, our first date at a Le Pain near campus.

જ જ જ

I look around the cute bakery and spot a glass jar with chocolaty cream jammed inside it.

"Organic hazelnut spread." I glance back at him and shake my head playfully. "A.k.a. knockoff Nutella," I continue.

An endearing smile spreads across his face before declaring, "The coffee is really good here."

∾ ∾ ∾

"Zara, Zara!" Daisy snaps me back into the present. "You need to get it together," Daisy demands sternly. "The alcohol affected you."

My head spins, and my heart hardens like lead. I squeeze my eyes shut and remember laying my head on his shoulder, followed by, "Just don't hurt me, okay?"

∾ ∾ ∾

I wake up the next morning and grab my pillow to scream. I wake up with this irresistible determination to eradicate the troubling, gloomy feeling I felt the night before. I tell myself I will never allow myself to feel that way again.

So, I buy the ticket.

SECOND TRIP TO NEW YORK

I hop off the train in a baby blue cashmere turtleneck (thank you, amazing vintage shop in Louisville), a gray scarf, pearl necklace, pleated gray skirt, fur-lined leggings, black leather boots, and a bluish, gray beret to top it all off. *Bonjour*.

Oh, people are walking fast here.

I walk faster than my normal pace and bubble with enthusiasm because I was in flipping New York! Or "New York, New York, New Yorrrk," as Alicia Keys eloquently puts it.

This is *my* New York experience. I can do whatever I want. I hit up Lane again because I need a bit of home to feel safe.

Lane awkwardly stands next to a concrete beam in Penn Station, waiting for me.

"Hey!" I shout with my beret bouncing around.

"You look super touristy." Lane chuckles.

What he means is, "You look super happy."

I am not saying New Yorkers are unhappy, but they put up a front. Smiling seems to be a sign of weakness. Oh, and they do not allow you to make eye contact for too long.

I mean, I get it, eye contact is the worst. It makes you create a bond with someone. Gasp.

That is why the New Yorker sits us in front of a TV at the bar where we reunite.

An hour prior to meeting the New Yorker at the bar, I slip on a black-and-gold dress in Lane's dorm.

"Are you sure you want to do this, Zara?" he mumbles.

"Yeah! Why not? I mean, I am in New York, and we have a lot of chemistry."

"Where are you guys meeting? Let me walk you there." Lane follows.

"I asked him if he wanted to get dessert. You know, since we already had dinner. But . . ."

"But?" he questions.

"But he wants to meet at this stupid bar," I admit.

"Maybe you shouldn't go," Lane persists.

"No, I want to go," I insist.

The New Yorker does not look at me as we speak. My body is facing him, and the direct eye contact is freaking him the hell out.

"I will get you a drink, what do you want?"

"I don't know, surprise me," I reply, with fake enthusiasm.

Ugh. Why does he want to intoxicate me? Drinking can be fun, but I was in the mood for ice cream.

After we left the bar, he wants to buy a bottle of wine for us.

"Maybe you shouldn't go" echoes into my head.

The whole time Lane is walking me to the bar, he tries to convince me the New Yorker may be a complete piece of shit. His tone is full of frustration and concern. I do not take what he says seriously because Lane does not know about the phone calls, text messages, and makeshift long-distance connection.

As we are waiting in line at CVS, I begin understanding Lane's frustration. The New Yorker has an agenda. He wants to get me drunk, like the first night we met.

That's when I know it is time to leave. I haven't gone to see him to get drunk; I want something deeper.

I want bacon maple donuts and intense eye contact.

I want something else; I want someone else. I text Lane. I had a feeling he would stay close. He shows up in less than two minutes. When I spot Lane's red hair, I say my goodbyes.

"I don't think I'm the right girl for you tonight, I'm sorry," I stammer.

The New Yorker rushes out to insult me, "They are usually out of beer around this time at the frats."

I pull his ass aside to set him straight.

"Number one, I am not going to a frat house. Number two, you don't need alcohol to enjoy yourself. I mean, for goodness' sake, I asked you to get dessert with me, and you took me to a bar. How does that look? Number three, I have absolutely no obligation to go with you."

His eyes wide with fear, his bravado breaks down. He apologizes profusely and assures me his authentic intentions are not to fool me. He pulls the right heartstring when he asks, "Do you even like me?"

Yes, I like you. Why do you think I met up with you?

He stumbles more and gives me a bogus excuse about the dessert.

"Why don't we just hang out at my apartment? We don't have to do anything. We can just watch a movie," he suggests.

My arms remain crossed. *Movie my ass.*

"I don't think so," I respond.

The Inevitable Loss of Innocence

"Come on, I thought we could take turns visiting each other. You come to New York this month, I go to DC the next. I like you, Zara."

My arms uncross, and I sigh. "Fine, but just one movie."

Kid you not, I'm planning on making him watch that entire movie.

Then an hour into the movie, he gently kisses me on the head. It's foolish, but I kiss him back. However, I quickly take note that he's a lot more aroused than I am. Things don't feel right.

He grabs my waist and lays me on my back. I force him to give me eye contact at that point.

After five seconds of eye contact, he remarks, "You're so cute."

Before I respond, I take a deeper look into his eyes. They aren't soft; they are sad.

"There is a lot of sadness in your eyes…Someone must have really hurt you," I murmur.

He responds with a weak smile and half-hearted chuckle.

"I think you're wrong. I think I am a happy person."

Oh, no, baby, you are happy, or you aren't.

I know my eyes do not love him after that. They aren't my favorite color. They aren't soft. And no, I do not jab my finger to feel it, but I can still feel it in my bones.

Eerie, frigid chills sliver through my bones.

Then…I close my eyes. I close them and shake my head and desperately try to wake up from this terrible dream.

All those text messages, all those lies. So many thoughts are cluttering my mind.

Why have I come to his apartment? Why have I come to New York? I wonder where Blaze's sister likes to write.

☙ ☙ ☙

My head would turn from side to side as I squeeze my eyes shut.

"Look at me. Look at me as if you want it," he demands.

I do not want it. I do not want sex. I want love.

MESSAGE I HAVE FOR
THE NEW YORKER

When you have a daughter, I want you to look at her beautiful, shiny eyes. The ones that never stay still and constantly wander from one corner of the room to another. Notice how she gently bats her eyelashes against them as she gets sleepy around 8:00 p.m.

Now imagine a guy aggressively telling her to shift those eyes toward his and to look at him "as if she wants it." Look at your daughter's shiny, chirpy eyes, and imagine a guy telling her to look at his miserable, dull eyes. Imagine that guy coercing her to look at him *as if* she wants it.

She will mean the world to you. Before you know it, she will graduate as senior class president, and you will gleam with pride and admiration. She will look at the crowd and lock eyes with you. Those shiny brown eyes will wander from one corner of the room to another. Notice how she gently bats her eyelashes as she looks down at her speech.

Now imagine her eyes looking at her cell phone screen as her angsty fingers slam against it, her heart pounding frantically and echoing harshly into her ear, fear rushing through her veins, and she will desperately need help.

She will text a boy she thinks cares about her. The boy with the miserable, dull eyes. The boy that told her she worries too much and that she should just have fun for once. She tells him how uncomfortable she feels in the room she's in, that she feels like she is in danger.

"Sorry, I can't help you. Nothing matters until finals are over," he responds. A piece of paper and letter claim to be more important than your daughter.

Her heart will drop to the floor. *Nothing* in big, black letters will cloud the room with darkness. This darkness will seep into her skin, and goose bumps will follow.

A boy told your daughter she does not matter, that her safety does not matter. Just remember, that boy is you.

TRUST

Whom do you trust? Why do you trust them? These questions should be answered without hesitation.

You have known them for a while, right?

You can always call them when you need them, right?

You thoroughly enjoy their presence, right?

Trusting people feels good. I just want to feel good in college.

But you forget to be wise when you focus on feeling good.

After I leave the New Yorker's apartment, I feel disgust. But when Lane picks me up, I tell him the stuff that amuses. Of course, I neglect the disturbing moments and stress the moments I make a statement.

The moments I give him a piece of my mind.

The moments I have power.

I was rewriting the story...Rather than being the victim, I was the perpetrator.

I throw the New Yorker in flames rather than drowning in despair.

"Oh, and then I told him how sad his eyes were, and...I...I gave a loud yawn and said, 'You know, I am exhausted. I will go now. I need to go get some sleep'," I rewrite.

"Hahaha! *Wow*, waste his time 2016! That is amazing," Lane applauds.

Lane is in awe. He exclaims I am his new idol. When I go back to his dorm, we smoke hookah with these random friends and amuse them, too.

One insists, "You should write a book about your life. People try to make up stories that are half as enticing as yours."

The following day I dedicate to myself. I walk around Manhattan by myself. I showcase my New Yorker strut and blend right in.

Walking alone through the streets of New York with your favorite tunes humming in your ears proves liberating.

After my walk, Lane shows me a ton more places. I feel the symptoms of exhaustion, but Lane insists I stay up.

His insistence is odd, but I don't read too much into it.

"Coffee, coffee, coffee," he suggests several times.

Around one in the morning, I'm virtually sleepwalking. "I should rest, Lane...I have to wake up early for my train tomorrow."

So I slip on some sheep-printed fleece pajama pants and a purple silky top.

When I get to the edge of the bed, Lane steps closer to me and pushes his body against mine.

"Move, Lane! I'm trying to fix the bed!"

The dramatic shift in tone does not faze him.

From my perspective, he seems to move slower, and his breathing becomes heavier. After a few seconds of shock, I release from his hold, slip into bed, and squeeze my eyes shut.

"Okay, good night!" I say.

The Inevitable Loss of Innocence

What the hell is going on?

Rather than respond, he hovers in silence and stares.

What does he want from me?

"Coffee coffee coffee," echoes in my head.

My heart pumps blood faster, and I do not know what is going through his mind.

Why isn't he letting me rest?

An eerie silence follows until he *finally* packs his stuff and leaves.

I wait five seconds after the door closes and rush to turn on the lights.

I change in ten seconds and pack my stuff.

My *angsty fingers slam against my cell phone screen.*

My *heart frantically pounds and echoes harshly in my ear.*

My *mind does not know whom to* trust.

I plead with the security guard at the front desk for my ID.

"I'm sorry, miss, but the student who checked you in has to sign you out," the stupid cop establishes.

"But I feel uncomfortable with him and don't know what he will do to me!" I exclaim.

I check my phone to see a message from him, exactly three minutes after he left.

"Where are you?" he texts.

Why has he come back so quickly?

I would've been all alone, in a stranger's bed, in complete darkness.

"Sir, please, my Uber thing will be here any minute! I need to leave!"

"Miss, I'm sorry, you could just leave your ID," he rationalizes.

I do.

I run outside and count down the seconds until the Uber got there.

Breath vapor blocks my vision as I anxiously look for the car.

"Come on, come on, come on!" I scream.

Finally, a black Volkswagen shows up, and I slam the door shut.

So many emotions are rerunning through my body as my legs begin shaking uncontrollably.

"You're going to the train station, right? I put it in right, right?"

"Yes, ma'am, no worries," he assures.

I run out of the car upon arrival, and the moment I see a flood of people, fear spikes into my bloodstream. Now I know how Snow White felt in the "far into the forest" scene.

Everything becomes blurry, and everything seems to spin. Thankfully, I spot a black man in a police uniform and run toward him.

"Help, sir, I need help. I need to get to Washington, DC. I need to change my ticket because I don't feel safe here. This boy, he pretends to be my friend, and then he just...his eyes. He pushed against me. He..." I hyperventilate, and a vicious ring in my ear follows.

"Ma'am, calm down, let's go to the office. Did he sexually assault you?"

"No! That's why I'm here. I need to leave, I need help, I..."

I run out of breath, and my throat locks up.

"Have some water, Miss." The police officer hands me a cup of water.

I crunch the plastic cup in my hand and sip on the water.

"Now, ma'am, if you want to report an assault, I will need more details. What was his name? Where did this happen? Are you okay? Do you need to see a medical expert?"

I almost choke on the water when he says "medical expert." I'm almost positive my mom has access to all my medical information. Therefore, I lie:

"You know, I am really overreacting. Nothing happened to me. I think it was all part of a dream. My neocortex can be insane." I chug the rest of the water and finish with, "I am sorry for the drama. Thank you. Bye."

My hands do not stop shaking until I board the Amtrak. Exhaustion overcomes my body when I sit in the comfy seat. I force myself to keep my eyes open.

The moment I doze off, my body violently pushes forward, hitting the seat in front of me.

The train suddenly stops.

Zara Macias

"Sorry, ladies and gentlemen, we seem to have hit a deer and will experience a delay. Sorry for the inconvenience and thank you for your patience."

That's when I lose it.

A train has crushed the delicate, dainty, delusional deer.

I am the deer.

He is the train.

DISTRICT 1

The brilliant Suzanne Collins describes in the *Hunger Games*:

It's to the Capitol's advantage to have us divided among ourselves. Another tool to cause misery in our district. A way to plant hatred between the starving workers [of the Seam] and those who can generally count on supper and thereby ensure we will never trust one another.

In sharp contrast to the starving worker, White University served elaborate hors d'oeuvres and cucumber water at this "Women in Office" talk with a ZNN moderator.

One lady flaunts her bright-red leather coat and diamond rings on every finger. Another has a sharp black Burberry suit and cashmere turtleneck.

Nothing compares to the fierce determination of White University professors and speakers however. They tuck their fangs and slick their hair back into tight ponytails.

It's time to solicit funds for the tributes…

I, the starved worker—I mean *student*—get near the fresh mozzarella balls, and my mouth begins to water. As I reach for a plate, my anxiety spikes and I question *what the fuck* I am doing there.

Am I allowed to be here?

Do I belong here?

Is this free?

Where am I? Who am I?

"Ladies and gentlemen! Well, mostly ladies…The talk will begin in two minutes."

I put the plate back quickly and rush to the front row.

The Inevitable Loss of Innocence

The ZNN gets comfortable in her seat and asks the speakers, "Funding, right?"

The speakers smile wide and wink.

Long story short, the pitch is extraordinarily emotional. We are in an apocalyptic reality, and the only way to save our souls is to write a fat check...and the ladies in the elegant wear do.

Thereby ensuring we will never trust one another.

GOING BACK TO DISTRICT 12

The moment the plane lands, I feel an *immense* wave of relief. I am no longer in DC or New York but my good ole Kentucky home. I convinced myself seeing the Christmas lights in New York would be unparalleled, but there's nothing more soothing than the soft embrace of a mother's arms.

Like a warm embrace, Kentuckians ask you how your family is doing, not what they do for a living. Your preferred college basketball team proves more relevant than your social class. Cars drive slowly and play soft tunes. Kentucky has a heart. Kentucky has a delicate softness to it. Kentucky is home.

Here, I have the privilege of being surrounded by people who truly care about my well-being. Despite the change of scenery, I can't shake off the roller coaster of emotions I have locked inside me.

∽ ∽ ∽

January 3, 2017, 8:30 p.m.

I drive my 2005 Ford Focus in the pouring rain.

Then..."She Will Be Loved" by Maroon 5 comes on the radio.

My eyes water, and I feel a big *weight*.

WEIGHT

You know the thing that sinks deep into your shoulders

The tension that lingers

Zara Macias

You know the thing that knocks the wind out of your stomach

The tension that lingers

You know that thing that pushes you

The tension that lingers

You know the thing that pushes you *hard*

The tension that lingers

You *know* the thing that causes you to skate, dance, pray, shout, *and* scream.

The. Tension. That. Lingers.

You.

You, Blaze, you. I've gotten involved with another boy to forget about you. It is stupid and immature, but it's what I've done. I want the rush of dopamine and the intense euphoria. I want to feel wanted. I need to be needed. Now I'm crying hysterically in the pouring rain, thinking about you, the innocence associated with you. I don't want to lose you.

REVISITING BLAZE

February 3, 2017, 7:15 p.m.

Knock, knock.

His face illustrates confusion, skepticism, and anger all at the same time.

"Hey...," I muddle.

He continues to look at me for a few seconds, and I suggest, "Do you want to come out here, or is it okay if I come in?"

"You can come in," he says softly.

"Okay, thanks..."

Blaze immediately walks over to his bed, sits down, and leans against the headboard with his arms crossed. My presence is not delightful or heartwarming. His body language reveals he's on the defense.

To cut through the tension, I express, "I just wanted to say I hope this semester is treating you well...just everything...I hope all is well."

"You talked a lot of shit about me, Zara. That is why I was not doing well."

It takes me back. I would never spread rumors or tarnish his reputation viciously. What does he mean by "a lot of shit"?

"Well, yes...Maybe I vented to people I confided in, but I would never tell a bunch of strangers. Maybe I should be more conscious of where I said the things, but look, I was angry, I didn't have closure . . ."

"You should have come to me if you wanted closure," he barks.

Yeaaah, I should go to the person who broke me to fix me.

"I was angry, and when we are angry, sometimes we say things we don't mean. I am sorry."

He nods and then responds, "That's valid."

I could have lashed out. I could have said, *Yes, I talked shit because you treated me like shit, you stupid piece of shit! You broke my heart! You promised me you wouldn't hurt me, and then you did it anyway! You picked me up and swung me around, and then you threw me on the ground abruptly without warning!*

"How's Hannah?" he follows (Hannah is roommate No. 2).

It's three of us in approximately 150 square feet.

"She's good...Elena moved out."

"Yeah, I know. I am great friends with Elena now..."

Ding, ding, ding! *Well, there is the source, ladies and gentlemen!*

My vengeful ex-roommate Elena tells him everything I've said to her in confidence. I don't get this girl—this girl and her unlimited credit card.

Again, I could have lashed out. I could have said, *Wow, really! She would tell you all the things I told her in confidence? Sorry she doesn't understand the concept of friendship! I mean, you guys are perfect for each other! You guys should go to Le Pain in your overpriced coats and have a grand time!*

Instead, I calmly respond, "That's good...I will keep this conversation short. I really hope you are doing well, and I'm always here if you need someone to talk to..."

It takes him aback. His eyes are wide with surprise.

Then he responds, "That's really cool of you, Zara. Thanks."

Blaze admires the "real." In the past, he'd complain about all the "fake" people at White University.

I give him a half-hearted smile and wish him a good night with poise.

"Good night, Zara," he says in a strange, somewhat monotone voice.

I close the door and walk down the hall with my head held high and take a sharp turn into the girls' bathroom.

Daisy, with her typical sexy silky top, waits anxiously.

"So?" she asks eagerly.

I immediately start bawling my eyes out, and she wraps her arms around me. With tears in my eyes, I laugh and mimic Daisy, "Zara, Zara! You need to get it together." I laugh with warm tears still fresh on my face.

"No, Zara, you're sober. And what you just did took a lot of balls. I mean, I could never do something like that. I admire you for that," Daisy applauds.

"Thank you for supporting me, girl," I respond. "Oh, and guess what?" I add.

"What?" she exclaims.

"It was Elena. Elena is why he stopped talking to me. She friggin' told everything I told her in private."

"What a bitch. And you know she probably made up a bunch of shit too," Daisy speculates.

"Maybe...Oh well, I did my part. If he wants anything to do with me, he can reach out to me."

CRAZY TIME IN HISTORY

It is 2017. The United States officially inaugurates a hateful Cheeto in chief, and emotions are wild. I am constantly trying to wrap my mind around the reality of our situation. Not to mention my international relations major is falling apart in front of my eyes.

"Make America Great Again"—yeah, more like "Make America completely oblivious to the realities of globalization, massive income inequality, and the importance of human decency."

Unfortunately, those words don't fit well on a baseball cap.

THE HISTORY BUFF

February 17, 2017

"You should meet History Buff," Mel contemplates.

"Oh really, why?" I ask.

"He is a history major. I think you'll like him."

"Yeah, maybe," I respond.

Fast-forward one week and I hear a knock on my door.

It's Mel.

"Hey, Me—" Before I can finish, she interrupts.

"Hey, Zara, I am in a bit of a rush, but here is History Buff's number." She hands me a pink sticky note with his name and number.

"Wait, don't you think that's weird? Just texting him out of the blue? Shouldn't you introduce him to me or something?" I hesitate.

"I don't know, I guess, but gotta run! Do what you want with it!"

She rushes down the hall, and I sigh dramatically before looking down at the pink sticky note.

I walk over to my bed and jump on top of it. I close my eyes and wave the hot pink sticky note around with frustration.

History Buff…

I slap the paper on the desk next to me and stare at the ceiling.

Hah, maybe we can talk about McCarthyism…That's relevant… Or the Civil Rights movement…Maybe even about Teddy friggin' Roosevelt…Such a character…

I sit up and stare at my deep-blue nails.

"Or I could stop obsessing over the historical parallels of our current political climate and take a deep bath into blissful ignorance..."

What the hell, I will just text him.

It doesn't mean I have to marry him or anything...

So, I text him, and we *reeeally* hit it off and schedule coffee that same night.

(I know, fuck my life.)

We both order hot chocolate because we are both too fidgety and nervous to drink coffee that late in the evening.

We talk and talk and talk and talk.

It is an instant connection—Southern boy and Southern girl fascinated with American history, particularly American political history.

We talk about the disturbing realities of White University: the lack of compassion, the lack of community, but the paradoxical assertions of "open-mindedness" and "inclusion."

On our walk back, he alerts me, "I have to watch this movie for my film class."

I nonchalantly follow, "Oh, can I watch with?"

I take him back and nervously fixate on where we will watch the film. I nonchalantly offer my hall's lounge.

My friend Lola is in the lounge and keeps a close eye. As I grab the HDMI cord, Lola asks me to meet outside my room and proceeds to gossip in her beautiful Puerto Rican accent, "He *liiikes* you, Zara. He was fixing his hair in his camera."

The Inevitable Loss of Innocence

I roll my eyes and express, "Ay, Lola, that's how those boys are."

I go back into the lounge and connect the TV.

Suddenly, my computer screen saver of Agua Azul pops up (an angelic waterfall in Palenque, Chiapas [Mexico]).

He marvels at the picture, and I reminisce, "You know, when I went there, I climbed these steps. I climbed and climbed until I was on the very top of the waterfall, and the view…the view was breathtaking. I wish I could go back…" My voice cracks. "It's just hard to be here sometimes…" I exhale.

He instantly embraces me and whispers, "I know."

After this vulnerable moment, we try to watch the film, but it is clear we both lack the focus to do so. There is so much emotion, so much energy in the room.

I rest my head on his chest and hear his heart beat faster and faster.

So, I go for it.

I grab his shirt and hold a passionate kiss, and it speeds up; it speeds up quickly. He reaches under my sweater dress and pushes his body above mine on the couch.

I don't know why, but I have the desire to cry.

I don't know why I take him into my room.

I don't know why we lie on our sides and look into each other's eyes.

"Who are you?" I whisper.

He smiles, kisses me one last time, and leaves.

A tear leaves my eye as I am left with loneliness.

֍ ֍ ֍

I would write about our trips to the museums and yet another fantasy I try to create, but he leaves.

Two weeks after the hot chocolate, I text him, wishing him a sunny spring break.

"Ha, I left Thursday."

Ha, you left. Ha, you left without saying goodbye. Ha, you got with a girl when you went back home. Ha, your mom posted pictures of you two...looking into her eyes...her soft ebony eyes.

Ha...I'm such a fool...

ABOUT ZARA MACIAS

Zara Macias, founder of ZDM Writing, is a Mexican Kentuckian writer, consultant, and social change champion. Zara holds a BA in Political Science with a track in Global Politics and International Affairs.

She wrote this book in the hopes that it will find the right reader and activate change around glossy narratives and untold truths.

She's quenched (some of) her thirst for social change by spending time learning advocacy methods at the ACLU Advanced Advocacy Institute; representing her hometown of Louisville, Kentucky, at the American Committee on Foreign Relations Young Leaders Initiative (ACFR YLI); and pioneering an Equity, Diversity, & Inclusion (EDI) in the most rural Kentucky food bank while serving on the national Feeding America EDI advisory committee.

Made in United States
Orlando, FL
30 May 2024